Aunt Bella's Cat

Written and illustrated by

Dee Shulman

You do not need to read this page - just get on with the book!

First published in Great Britain by Barrington Stoke Ltd
10 Belford Terrace, Edinburgh EH4 3DQ
Copyright © 2001 Dee Shulman
Illustrations © Dee Shulman
The moral right of the author has been asserted in
accordance with the Copyright, Designs and
Patents Act 1988
ISBN 1-84299-007-1
Printed by Polestar AUP Aberdeen Ltd

Meet the Author and Illustrator
Dee Shulman

What is your favourite animal?
Cat (of course!)
What is your favourite boy's name?
Mr Tumnus
What is your favourite girl's name?
Verucca Salt
What is your favourite food?
Birthday cake
What is your favourite music?
My son on the violin and
my daughter on the guitar
What is your favourite hobby?
Encouraging our cats to take some
exercise

For Nicola, Bash Bash, Beermoth and Bluebell

Contents

Chapter 1
Aunt Bella

"Oh, NO! Not Aunt Bella!" I wail at Mum.

"Really Kate, I can't believe I'm hearing this. Most children would give anything to spend a day with a filmstar like Bella!"

"Why can't I go to Dad's? You promised."

Mum sighs. "Your Dad phoned last night to say he couldn't take you after all."

"What about Emma?"

"Emma's mum says they're busy this weekend."

"Well why do *you* have to work this Saturday? It's not fair. You're *always* at the hospital."

"Look, Kate, it's really lucky your Aunt Bella's in England right now and that she's agreed to have you. You know how little you get to see her."

"*Never* would be too often. Anyway, why isn't she in Hollywood making movies?"

"She's just back for the British opening of her latest film. Then she'll be off again. Now run along and get your stuff together, she'll be here in a minute."

"What? She's coming to pick me up?" I gasp.

"Yes – isn't that lovely of her. She's taking you to a show or something."

It is the *or something* that worries me. With Bella nothing is simple. When I was five she took me on a lovely trip to a farm *or something*. Only it was a *health* farm and we had to walk around all day with yoghurt on our faces.

When I was seven she took me to a fair *or something*. Only it was a *book* fair, and Bella was there to sell her book of Beauty Tips.

So what will a show *or something* turn out to be?

I stomp off to my room, and look around for things to take with me. I pack up some books, a Gameboy, a packet of Rolos, my Discman, and four CDs. Then I settle down to wait.

Chapter 2
The Long Wait

Aunt Bella is never on time. For some reason this always seems to take Mum by surprise.

Mum phones Aunt Bella's house, her mobile and her car phone ... no answer. Her agent can't help, nor can her press office. So Mum ends up phoning the hospital to grovel about how late she's going to be for work.

"Oh well – it looks as if I'll just have to come to the hospital with you, Mum," I say, trotting happily to the front door.

Mum hasn't let me come to the hospital with her ever since I tripped and sent a trolley piled with bed-pans crashing into some top consultant on his ward round.

"We'll give her one more minute," Mum says desperately.

Guess what? In the 58th second, there is a loud ring on the doorbell. Something tells me it isn't the postman. I open the door and am suddenly engulfed in fur, perfume and jangly earrings.

"Katerina, darling," gushes Aunt Bella. "Goodness, what are you wearing? Run along and get dressed, child, we're going out."

"But Aunt Bella ..."

"That gorgeous little dress I sent you for your birthday would be perfect."

"BBBut ..."

Luckily, Mum is beginning to snort with fury. "Bella! I am very, *very* late for work. The dress you gave Kate when she was eight no longer fits, and if I stand here much longer my patients will be dying of old age. Have a lovely day both of you and see you tonight. Good*bye*."

She steers us out of the front door and strides towards her car.

"Oh well," says Aunt Bella and gives me that look which says, 'how did a beautiful woman like me end up having to look after a disgusting little squit like you'. I stand on the doorstep and watch forlornly as my only hope for a better day gets into her car and drives off.

"Bye, Mum!"

Chapter 3
The Abyssinian Prince

"Come along then Katerina, I'll introduce you to Bashir!"

"Who's Bashir?" I ask.

"My Abyssinian Prince!"

Oh no, she's got a prince in the car. And I can't speak Abby-sin-yan.

A driver jumps out of Aunt Bella's limo and opens the door for me. I peer in nervously. Inside is a tall man with long hair and earrings. The car has very dark windows, but he is wearing sunglasses. He must be the Abyssinian Prince *in disguise*!

I do my best bow and mumble, "Hello your Highness ..." I'm interrupted by a rather unpleasant squawk of laughter. It is coming from Aunt Bella.

The tall man starts to snigger too.

"No! No! Jez is my secretary, Katerina darling. My Abyssinian Prince is in the basket there."

That's when I notice a green wicker basket on the seat next to Jez. Bella reaches over and throws open the lid.

"But ... the Abyssinian Prince is a cat?"

"Of course! My magnificent Bashir!"

"Oh – he's beautiful!" I put my hand out to stroke Bashir, but Jez pushes it away.

"I wouldn't do that if I were you!" Jez says. He has a deep, slow American accent. "That cat may look beautiful but he's vicious. Look ..." He holds up his hands, which are crisscrossed with scratches and bites.

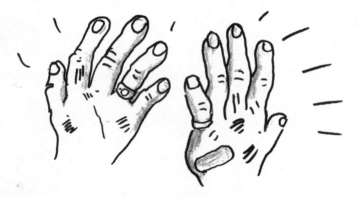

Jez looks into the basket and frowns. Bashir lifts his head and hisses, baring his teeth and fluffing up his fur. Then he starts to growl like a dog!

"See what I mean?" says Jez.

"Will you stop being so rude about my Prince, Jez," complains Aunt Bella, "and move along for Katerina to sit down."

I sit down next to the basket and sneak a look at Bashir. Through half-closed yellow eyes, Bashir stares back at me. He is the most amazing cat I have ever seen. He has this thick fur and it's a lovely, powdery blue-grey colour. I sit there watching him. He begins to make a rich purring sound.

The driver clears his throat.

Ahem, Madam— I think we'd better get moving or we'll be late for the show!

"Heavens, you're right – The Show!"

"What sort of show is it exactly, Aunt Bella?"

"Didn't anyone tell you, Katerina?" Bella settles herself into her seat, "We're going to The National Cat Show!"

"Cat show?"

"Yes! It's where they have judges to find the most beautiful cats. My little Bashir is going to win us some lovely rosettes, aren't you darling!"

"If anyone can get near him!" says Jez with a snigger, clicking up his seat belt.

The driver starts up the engine and as we pull away, this really weird thing happens. Bashir suddenly springs out of his basket towards me.

"LOOK OUT!" yells Jez.

But for some reason I'm not afraid. I put out my arms to catch Bashir. He looks me straight in the eye, then snuggles down into my lap. He gives me a little lick, closes his eyes and begins to purr.

Even Aunt Bella looks shocked.

"I've never seen him do *that* before. The cat must be sickening for something!"

Chapter 4
The Cat Show

Bashir stays curled up on my lap all the way to the cat show, purring softly, and stretching out the bits he wants to be tickled. I don't want this journey ever to end.

But it does. The car slows down to a stop, and the driver jumps out to open our doors. Aunt Bella sends Jez off with all the pedigree papers to collect the entrance tickets. Then she shoves me out of the car, puts on a pair of thick, leather gloves, grabs Bashir and steps out into crowds of people.

Most of them turn out to be her fans. She hands Bashir over to me, and gets on with what she's best at: being adored, signing autographs and flashing her dazzling smile at the cameras.

Soon Jez comes dashing back and pulls
Bashir and me towards the end of a long
line of people. We wait for ages, while Aunt
Bella enjoys her adoring public. At last
we're at the front of the queue.

"Right," says a vet, "let's have a look at
you!" and he puts out his hands to take
Bashir from me. There is a great snarling
and scratching as Bashir refuses to be
taken.

"You see Kate," whispers Jez, "this is the
Bashir the rest of us know and love!"

In the end the vet lets me hold Bashir while he does the medical check. Phew! We can move to the next stage: Registration.

If it wasn't for Bashir I would be well bored, but he's really good fun. He climbs onto my shoulders and down my back and then winds himself around my legs before lying down on his back for a tummy tickle!

We're so busy playing that I don't even notice Jez has got to the front of the queue until he comes and waves all the papers under my nose.

All done! We can go through at last!

He drags Aunt Bella from her fans, and a man with an official badge leads us into this massive hall. It's full of rows and rows of cages.

We stop at cage 258 and the official opens the door. Bashir is *not* happy to be put inside.

Aunt Bella leans against the cage cooing at Bashir, while I try not to get swept away by the crowd. Some people are getting on with sorting out their cages and cats. Others turn out to be Aunt Bella's fans who hover nearby, giggling and pointing.

Suddenly I become aware of someone who is looking at Aunt Bella in a very different way. She is a mean-faced woman and she is whispering to two men who don't look a bit like cat lovers. All three stare in our direction.

"Aunt Bella!" I say urgently, but she is busy signing autographs for two old ladies.

One of the old ladies peeks into Bashir's cage. "Ooh! He's an Abyssinian Blue! They are a special favourite of Judge Grumpolo, aren't they, Ruby?"

Her friend nods excitedly. "He's one of the most famous judges, you know. It's a great honour to have him here today!"

Then she squeaks with delight. "Look there he is, over there!"

I am just beginning to relax when Rat-Face comes right over and stares straight into Bashir's cage.

Bashir stares back. His fur stands up and he starts a low sort of growl.

"Aunt Bella!" I tug at her sleeve.

"Not now, child," she hisses, "I can't hear what they're saying ..."

WOULD ALL OWNERS PLEASE LEAVE THEIR CATS, AND MAKE THEIR WAY UP TO THE BALCONY. THE JUDGES ARE NOW READY TO BEGIN ...

Chapter 5
Kit-Nap

The crowd begins moving towards the side doors. Bella and Jez join the crush.

"AUNT BELLA!" I shout, but she doesn't hear. I look around. There are people everywhere, pushing and shoving. My instinct tells me to stay put and guard Bashir. But then I catch sight of Rat-Face right over by a balcony door. "Phew!" I

31

breathe, "She's leaving!" and let myself be swept away with the crowd.

As I reach the door, I just glance back towards Bashir's cage. "NO!" I gasp.

But at that moment the loudspeaker starts up again.

PLEASE CLEAR THE HALL AS FAST AS POSSIBLE. THE COMPETITION WILL BEGIN IN FIVE MINUTES...

I struggle back, against the flow of people, but by the time I get to Bashir's cage, the two men have gone.

So has Bashir!

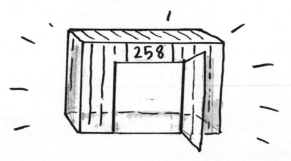

I look around, frantic. Where could they have taken him?

In panic, I scan the room. There's a fire exit door swinging shut. I take a chance and dart towards it.

By the time I get there, only a few people are left in the hall. I don't want to draw attention to myself so I slip quickly through.

The door opens out onto a long, empty corridor. I have no idea which way to go, so I stand there dithering. Then I hear something faint but familiar –

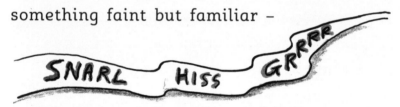

SNARL   HISS   GRRRR

Bashir!

I follow the sound as quietly as I can.

The snarls lead me along two more corridors, down a flight of steps, through some double doors – then CLUNK!

Silence.

What have they done to Bashir? I race round the next corner and find myself facing a huge metal door. Dragging it open, with all my strength, I just manage to squeeze through. CLUNK! The door slams shut behind me.

I stand facing an enormous car park. My heart sinks. They could be anywhere. They could even have driven away by now.

Stay calm, I tell myself, trying to think of a plan. Suddenly the door of a big red jeep flies open and I can hear spitting, snarling and swearing.

"Good old Bashir," I chuckle, as I dive for cover behind a blue van. Then I hear voices.

"I've had enough! You take the naffing animal. I'm not staying here to get clawed to bits. Couldn't we have drugged it anyway?"

"Couldn't risk getting the dose wrong. This cat's got to stay healthy. It's *big* money. You saw whose cat this is – it's that woman, Bella what's-her-name. She's famous ... and loaded. She'll pay thousands to get it back.

He lifts his hand to hit Bashir, but I can't watch. I leap out yelling "BASHIR!" But as I fling myself forward, I am suddenly grabbed from behind.

Chapter 6
Caught

Now things happen really fast.

The two men jump back into the jeep with Bashir and start up the engine. The blue van I've been hiding behind starts up too. I struggle to get away from the man who's holding on to me.

The jeep and van race towards the car park exit. I have begun to get really scared.

And ... (gulp) ...

I try to act brave. "There are guards at the gate. You'll never get away with it!" I squeak.

The man holding me just smiles. He's about to say something clever, when there's this crackling sound and he pulls a walkie talkie from his belt. All I hear him say is, "NO – I understand. Flush her out."

What does *that* mean? It doesn't sound very pleasant.

There's no way I'm going to wait to find out. While he's talking he's only holding on to me with one hand. I kick his ankle as hard as I can, then jerk myself out of his grip. He's still yowling with pain as I start to run.

I've just about made it back to the big metal door when he catches up with me.

"You're as wild as that cat!" he complains. "That really hurt!" and he rubs his ankle crossly.

"POLICE! HELP!" I shout again, but he puts his hand over my mouth.

"SHHH," he whispers, "I *am* the police! Officer Jarvis to be exact. And believe it or not I've just rescued you! We've been watching this gang for months. Those two men are armed and dangerous."

"Poor Bashir! What will they do to him?"

"Nothing! Your cat is safe. There were four police officers in the blue van and they have just made an arrest. But we still have to flush out the boss – Nora Stote ..."

"You mean the rat-faced woman?"

"You've seen her? Would you recognize her again?"

"Of course I would!"

Officer Jarvis looks thoughtful. "Now then. I like to see a brave kid, and I like to see a tough kid. And I've seen that you're both of those. But ... jumping out on two armed robbers isn't brave or tough. It's stupid. You could have got yourself killed, and that wouldn't have helped the cat would it?"

I shake my head.

"But ... now I need you to do some real police work. Be part of the team. Nora Stote is on the balcony watching the cat show. She wants to be seen there, so no-one will suspect her of being involved in the kidnap. Now that the others are caught she could walk away, let them go to prison, and just find some more bad guys to do her work. So, we have to prove that she's involved. That is where you come in ..."

Chapter 7
The Plan

The next thing I know, I'm carrying a note that Officer Jarvis has written, up to the balcony. Luckily Rat-Face Stote is sitting right near the door and is easy to spot. All I have to do is give her the note, and hope she doesn't suspect anything.

She reads it and then says sharply, "Who gave you this?"

"Two men," I say, trying my best to look innocent. And I describe her partners. She gives me a hard stare, looks at the note again, mutters, "Idiots!" under her breath and leaves.

My bit's over and I breathe a sigh of relief.

Too soon. Rat-Face is back.

"Little girl," she hisses, and grabs my arm, "you'd better come with me!" and she drags me out the door.

My first thought is, *Cheek! I'm not a little girl. I'm an important member of a fearless police team!* But that thought is quickly replaced with, *Uh-oh! This isn't meant to be happening ...*

As we head for the car park, Rat-Face speaks, "I don't know where my ... er ... friends are. You'll have to show me."

We get through the big metal door and I stand on the step, wondering what to do now. I pretend to be working out exactly where I last saw them.

Then the kidnapper's red jeep screeches up to us and the passenger door swings open. "Quick, get in!" a man's voice whispers. Rat-Face doesn't hesitate. She lets go of me and disappears inside. The jeep speeds away.

I'm left standing on the step, confused. What just happened? Maybe Officer Jarvis isn't a real policeman. He wasn't wearing a uniform and he never showed me his badge. Maybe he's another of Rat-Face's men and I've just helped with their getaway!

And what about Bashir?

Chapter 8
Together Again

Suddenly I hear a familiar spitting and snarling sound. I turn around and coming towards me is Officer Jarvis with Bashir!

As soon as they get near, Bashir flies out of his arms into mine!

"Thank goodness for that," pants Jarvis as he nurses his scratched and bleeding hands.

"But the kidnappers just drove off!" I say.

"No, no – there were two of *our officers* in the jeep. We have just successfully arrested Nora Stote, thanks to you!"

I grin. Then I give Bashir a little kiss ...

Bashir! ... The show! ... The competition ...
Will we still be in time for the judging?

I rush into the hall and get Bashir back
in his cage seconds before Judge Grumpolo
gets there.

Phew! That was close.

Back on the balcony, Aunt Bella is easy to spot, as she has the usual gaggle of fans all around her. Jez glances up as I clamber across a whole row of people to join them.

Bored! Ha!

Chapter 9
The Champion

"Aunt Bella ... sorry I disappeared, but Bashir ..."

"Oh do stop wittering, Katerina. Look, the judging has finished. Come on darlings, let's go and count Bashir's rosettes!"

We trail behind as Aunt Bella rushes down the stairs.

Who's Mummy's little champion then?

"Aunt Bella ..." I start, but Jez interrupts.

"I am afraid Bella, my sweet, your Abyssinian Prince has won nothing at all!"

"Don't be absurd, Jez ..." Aunt Bella mutters, searching the cage for rosettes.

"But Aunt Bella," I try again, "Bashir had such a big shock, he probably ..."

Aunt Bella isn't listening. She is peering down at the floor. "They must have dropped off!" she says brightly. "On your knees, both of you. The rosettes will be on the floor somewhere ..."

We find several cat hairs

a five pence piece

and a strawberry Chewitt.

We don't find a single rosette.

"I'll soon have it sorted out!" Aunt Bella announces and she strides off towards the judge's table.

"Bella," Jez calls after her weakly, "I don't think ..."

But Aunt Bella's already halfway there. We trail miserably behind.

"Excuse me!" she says, tapping Judge Grumpolo on the shoulder, "My gorgeous Abyssinian Prince has no rosette on his cage. I must assume that this is a simple mistake which it will be easy to put right."

Judge Grumpolo frowns dangerously.

"Now, please be good enough to return to your cat, as we are about to give out the trophies ..." and he picks up the microphone to begin the prize-giving.

Judge Grumpolo is making two very big mistakes.

The first is that he thinks Aunt Bella will do as she is told. And the second is that he switches on the microphone. He just has time to say, "AHEM ..." into it when Aunt Bella gets started.

SIR!

Her voice echoes around the totally silent hall.

I BEG YOU TO TAKE ANOTHER LOOK AT MY POOR, UNFAIRLY SNUBBED BASHIR. I AM CERTAIN THE ROSETTE THAT SHOULD BE THERE IS MISSING. INDEED I WOULDN'T BE SURPRISED IF IT HADN'T BEEN STOLEN BY SOME LESS DESERVING CREATURE'S OWNER!

and she looks pointedly in the direction of the hairless cat.

Now Judge Grumpolo is not the sort of person you would normally feel sorry for. But as he stands there with his mouth opening and shutting helplessly, he looks a bit like a fish which has just been tipped out of its tank. Twitching slightly, he shuts his mouth, picks up his clipboard, and allows Aunt Bella to lead him off.

Chapter 10
Final Judgement

"Here he is!" Aunt Bella announces in triumph. "Isn't he beautiful?"

Judge Grumpolo looks through his notes. "Mmm ... ah ... yes ... Number 258?"

"Yes, yes!" says Bella eagerly.

"Mmm ... Let me see ... Abyssinian Blue ... the breed's a special favourite of mine as it happens ..."

"Yes I know that," says Aunt Bella smiling back at him, warmly.

"But ..." interrupts Judge Grumpolo, "This, I'm afraid is rather a pitiful example of an Abyssinian Blue."

"WHAT?" splutters Aunt Bella.

"REALLY!" explodes Bella. Then she adds under her breath, "and that coming from you!"

"The Abyssinian nose," continues Judge Grumpolo, "should come forward in a glorious curve. This cat's face is ... how can I describe it? It's ... squashy!"

"Don't listen to him, Bashir," says Bella, covering Bashir's ears with her hands.

"But of course, the final straw with *this* animal ..." Judge Grumpolo is fully in control now, "is his character." To prove his point he holds up a scratched and bitten hand.

"I could claim for damages if I chose!" he booms and looks around his audience who tut-tut in sympathy.

"Now, if I may proceed, we are running rather late ..." and he heads off towards the trophy table followed by a small crowd of officials.

Chapter 11
Arrest

"Come on!" commands Bella, "We are not staying at this ridiculous event a moment longer." And she sweeps us off towards the door.

Suddenly her way is blocked. Standing in front of her is Officer Jarvis with three policemen in uniform.

"What on earth is the meaning of this?" hisses Aunt Bella. The hall has gone quiet again. All eyes turn towards us.

"You must be aware of the kidnap attempt on your cat less than half an hour ago."

"What on earth are you talking about?" she splutters.

"Thanks to your niece, here ..." I feel myself going hot and pink, "and to her courage, skill and teamwork, we have been able to foil the kidnap and arrest all three criminals responsible!"

There's a huge cheer from the crowd.

Then suddenly I am surrounded by photographers and reporters!

The rest of the event is a blur of flashing cameras and questions.

Aunt Bella meanwhile offers interviews of her own:

"Katerina, honey-pie – come and be in a celebrity photo with me and Bashir!"

Chapter 12
A Visitor

The next morning I am sitting at the kitchen table, reading all about myself in the paper when there's this ring at the doorbell.

DING

DONG

KITNAPPED!

BELLA UPSTAGED!

KATE AND THE CATTHIEVES!

Reluctantly I put down the newspaper and go and answer it ...

THUMP! I am knocked over by something hard and green.

Dazed, I look up to see Aunt Bella whooshing past me, the green basket in her hand.

"Aunt Bella?" I croak, rubbing my elbow.

Aunt Bella stops, and turns.

She doesn't wait for an answer. "Never mind, darling. Now listen. Jez and I have got to fly back to Hollywood today, and my maid simply refuses to look after Bashir for me."

"Er ... What? Look after Bashir? Me? Y-Y-Y...YES!"

"Bless you, Sweetie. Must dash now – love to your mother. Bye ..."

As I stand on the doorstep watching Aunt Bella's limo disappear down the road, a sudden warm and glowing thought occurs to me.

There *is* something good about Aunt Bella after all. There is something truly *wonderful* about her. Something *lovable* and *cuddly* and *soft* and *special* ...

... BASHIR!

Barrington Stoke was a famous and much-loved story-teller. He travelled from village to village carrying a lantern to light his way. He arrived as it grew dark and when the young boys and girls of the village saw the glow of his lantern, they hurried to the central meeting place. They were full of excitement and expectation, for his stories were always wonderful.

Then Barrington Stoke set down his lantern. In the flickering light the listeners were enthralled by his tales of adventure, horror and mystery. He knew exactly what they liked best and he loved telling a good story. And another. And then another. When the lantern burned low and dawn was nearly breaking, he slipped away. He was gone by morning, only to appear the next day in some other village to tell the next story.

Barrington Stoke would like to thank all its readers for commenting on the manuscript before publication and in particular:

Lorenzo Aceto
Lucia Ariano
Kimberley Sarah Armitage
Nicola Bissett
Maddy Brook
Beatrice Brook-Farrell
Elliot Luke Brook-Farrell
Elizabeth Cook
Sue Davies
Joe Dobson
Daniel Falcon
Lucy Hurley
Mohammed Imran Hussein
Anita Jhingde
Matthew Johnson
Gail Macleod
Dominique MacNeil

Camilla Morris
Philippa Morris
Kyia Murray
Grace Naylor
Jade Phelan
Gillian Reeve
Michael Rinaldi
Kanishk Sharma
Molly Sheridan
Charlie Summerville
Hannah Swallow
Daniel Vassar
Pasquale Ventrone
Daniella Watson
Peter Webb
Terence Wilkinson
Rebecca Vigers

Become a Consultant!

Would you like to give us feedback on our titles before they are published? Contact us at the address or website below – we'd love to hear from you!

Barrington Stoke, 10 Belford Terrace, Edinburgh EH4 3DQ
Tel: 0131 315 4933 Fax: 0131 315 4934
E-mail: info@barringtonstoke.co.uk
Website: www.barringtonstoke.co.uk

If you loved this story, why don't you read . . .

Pompom

by Michaela Morgan

Have you ever wished you had a dog? Paul dreams of having a champion dog to improve his image. It will give him something to boast about and help him with the bullies. But things go badly wrong – or do they? Discover how Paul finds out that looks are not everything.

You can order this book directly from:
Macmillan Distribution Ltd, Brunel Road, Houndmills,
Basingstoke, Hampshire RG21 6XS
Tel: 01256 302699